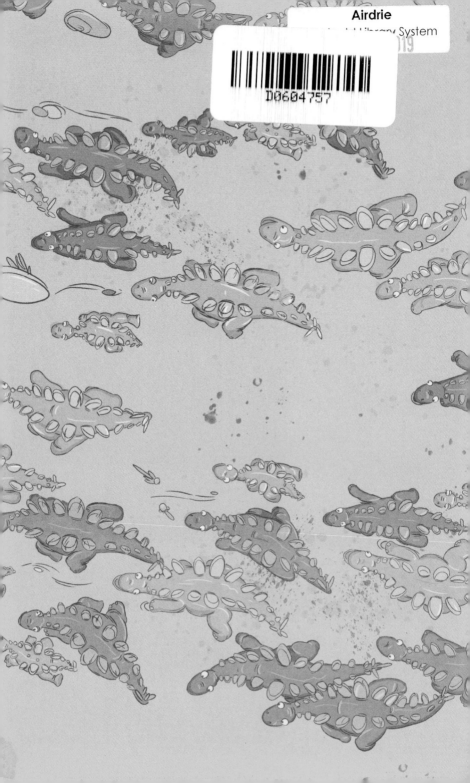

MICROSAURS
TINY-STEGO STAMPEDE

MICROSAURS

TINY-STEGO STAMPEDE

DUSTIN HANSEN

Fe
Ne

A FEIWEL AND FRIENDS BOOK

An imprint of Macmillan Publishing Group, LLC

175 Fifth Avenue, New York, NY 10010

MICROSAURS: TINY-STEGO STAMPEDE. Copyright © 2018 by Dustin Hansen.
All rights reserved. Printed in the United States of America by LSC
Communications, Harrisonburg, Virginia.

Our books may be purchased in bulk for promotional, educational,
or business use. Please contact your local bookseller or the Macmillan
Corporate and Premium Sales Department at (800) 221-7945 ext. 5442
or by e-mail at MacmillanSpecialMarkets@macmillan.com.

Library of Congress Control Number: 2017956991

ISBN 978-1-250-09032-4 (hardcover) / ISBN 978-1-250-09034-8 (ebook)

Book design by Liz Dresner

Feiwel and Friends logo designed by Filomena Tuosto

First edition, 2018

10 9 8 7 6 5 4 3 2 1

mackids.com

For young Charlie,
who will be surrounded by good words,
and his mother, who knows how to find them.

CHAPTER 1
THE THUNDERING HERD

"How do you hide a herd of stegosaurus?" Lin asked. She picked a long strand of grass, then started chewing on it as we sat in the big open field.

"Stegosauri," I said.

"Huh?" Lin said with a confused look on her face.

"I think the plural of *stegosaurus* is *stegosauri*," I explained.

"Well, right now it's more like zero-sauri. Are you sure they're in here already?" Lin asked.

"Sure, I'm sure. Professor Penrod let them go before he went exploring in Utah. He said, '*Danny, old boy, I've released a herd of new critters in the Microterium. Stegosauri, to be exact. I'm sure they'll get along just fine, but I would feel a whole lot better if you and Lin would check in on the new herd* and see if they're feeling hunky-dory,'" I said in my best Professor Penrod impression.

"Well, that sounds like him all right. But I still don't see any stegos. Maybe they're underground," Lin said.

"I doubt it. They're like bison of the Old West, or cows even. You know, grazers. I think if we keep looking in this grassy area we'll find them soon enough," I said. I tossed a stick to Bruno. He settled down next to me and began chewing it to bits.

"We've been looking forever. I just wish they'd give us a sign," Lin said, taking off her hat, which used to belong to Professor Penrod. She wiped her brow on the sleeve of her shirt. Then we heard a deep bellow behind us that literally shook the earth. Well, it shook the Microterium, that's for sure.

Lin and I looked at each other. Our mouths flopped open.

"What was that?" I asked.

"More like, *who* was that?" Lin said. "Let's go see."

Without waiting for my reply, Lin jumped on Zip-Zap's back, and in a flash, they zipped toward the noise. I quickly stuffed the rest of our lunch in my backpack, then climbed on Bruno. Zip-Zap and Lin were almost to the top of a little hill. Bruno did his best to keep up, but his stumpy legs were not built for sprinting.

Before Bruno and I reached the top of the hill, Zip-Zap and Lin came rushing back. Bouncing along on Zip-Zap, Lin waved her arms like crazy, her eyes so wide open it looked she'd seen a Microsaur ghost!

"Run! Turn around!" Lin shouted, but Bruno and I were frozen in our tracks.

The long neck of the largest Microsaur I've ever seen stretched out over the hill behind Lin. It was taller than a construction crane. His leather skin looked like tree bark, old and wrinkled, and his head was as wide as a minivan. He opened his mouth and let out another deep bellow, and the sound rumbled and trembled all the way down to the pit of my stomach. I knew I should be scared because I was directly in the path of a walking skyscraper, but I couldn't help but smile. He was the most amazing Microsaur I'd ever seen, and I've seen a lot of amazing Microsaurs.

Lin zipped by Bruno and me. "Danny! RUN! It's a stego stampede!"

I pulled my eyes from the long-necked Microsaur to the top of the hill just as three, then five, then more than twenty stegosauri charged over the hill. Their feet sounded like thunder as they rushed toward us, and I didn't have to tell Bruno to do anything. He spun around and burst down the hill, his stumpy legs churning faster than I ever thought possible.

But even though Bruno was trying his best, the stampede caught up to us in no time.

Stegosauri twice Bruno's size snorted and slobbered as they pounded the earth beneath them, stirring up a thick cloud of dust. I coughed and wheezed, then pulled my shirt up over my nose.

I tried with all my might to get Bruno to smash his way out of the stampede, but it was no use. We were totally caught up in the flow. The spiked tail of a big bull stego swooshed over my head, nearly turning me into a shish

kebab. We bumped into the rump of another stampeding Microsaur, and it would have sent me flying if my right shoe hadn't been twisted under Bruno's collar.

As I squinted through the dirt cloud, I saw my only hope for escape. A small pile of jagged boulders a few inches taller than Bruno jutted out of the grass. I leaned to the right with all the muscle I could muster and pulled my triceratops toward the rocky hiding spot. Bruno used his strong neck and bony crest to bully his way out of the herd. Then, as if he was reading my mind, he jumped over the rock pile and ducked behind it. I fell to the ground next to him and rolled up into a ball by his side.

Hundreds of thundering stegosaurus feet stomped around us. Some even climbed the little pile of rocks and jumped right over our heads as we ducked for cover. The stampede came to an end as the massive body of the long-necked dinosaur slowly cast his shadow over Bruno and me. The massive Microsaur bellowed again, and dust and tiny pebbles tumbled down on us as we crouched in our hiding spot.

The stego stampede faded into a dust cloud, making its way down the hill. I was about to tap on my Invisible Communicator to call for Lin, when she and Zip-Zap poked around the edge of the pile of jagged rocks.

"Danny? Are you okay?" she asked.

I stood up and checked to make sure all my parts were still attached. I was so shaken by the experience that I honestly wasn't sure. "Everything looks okay," I said. Then the two of us shared a huge grin.

"That . . . was . . . AMAZING!" we both said at the same time.

"Did you see the big one?" Lin asked.

"Of course! He's pretty hard to miss," I said.

"And there must have been a hundred stegos," Lin said.

"At least. Maybe more!" I said, filled with excitement.

"We have a big problem, Danny. How are we going to name them all?" Lin asked. "Holy moly—it's going to be impossible!"

While I agreed with Lin that it was going to be tough to name all the stegos, there was something else worrying me.

"I think we might have a bigger problem than that. Look at the grass, Lin. It's totally ruined. They smashed it flat," I said.

"Whoa. That's not good," she replied with panic in her voice, and I could tell she was as worried as me.

"We have to do something about this. Look at that." I pointed to a pile of sticks that was once a grove of trees. "We can't let them just run around and smash everything," I said.

"True, but what?" Lin asked.

Just before I blurted out a totally overcomplicated idea that included underground laser wire, motion detectors, nets, and flashing lights, Lin chimed in with the most obvious and perfectly simple idea ever.

"I guess we could build a fence," she said. "You said they were like cows. Cows stay inside of fences all the time."

"Of course. Why didn't I think of that?" I said. "We could build it out of the same blocks we used to build the Fruity Stars Lab 3.0. I have plenty left over back home."

Lin climbed back on Zip-Zap, then straightened her hat. "Well, come on, then, Danny. This fence isn't going to build itself," she said. She *yahoo*'ed her best cowgirl yelp, then cheered as Zip-Zap ran toward the Fruity Stars Lab.

Bruno dipped lower so I could easily jump on his back, but then he just stood there waiting.

"Come on, Bruno. Let's go," I said. The big Microceratops huffed a big breath but didn't move an inch. "What's wrong? Let's go."

Bruno huffed again, and I knew what he was waiting for. "Oh, okay. I get it," I said. I let out a loud and very cowboyish *YIPEE ki-YAY!* and Bruno thundered down the hill after Lin and Zip-Zap.

CHAPTER 2
FENCING FOR BEGINNERS

On my ride back to the Fruity Stars Lab 3.0, I had plenty of time to think about Lin's fence plan. It sounded easy, but I knew from experience that things that sounded easy in the Microterium ended up being . . . well, not so easy.

Something wasn't quite right, but I couldn't figure it out. By the time we arrived at the lab,

Lin was waiting for us and feeding one of her
specially made Microbite energy pellets to Zip-Zap.

"Howdy, slowpokes," Lin said with a nod of
her hat.

"We're slow but sturdy. Just the way I like it," I
said as I slid from Bruno's back.

"Here you go. Fuel up, buddy," Lin said as she rolled a Microbite to Bruno. He started munching on it right away.

"So, Lin. I've been thinking," I said.

"Of course you have," she said. "I'm not surprised."

"One time I was watching an old cowboy movie with my dad. The cowboys built a fence for their cows, but as soon as they finished putting up the last post, the herd smashed it to bits. And these were only cows. We're talking about building a fence for a bunch of stegos that make cows look like kittens. I'm not sure a fence is going to be enough," I said.

"Maybe the cowboys should have built a fence with PIBBs," Lin suggested. "We can build it as high, and strong, as we want."

"Yeah, I guess so. But there are more problems that are bugging me, too," I said.

"Like what?" Lin said.

"Well, for one. We don't know where the herd of stegos is going to be. So, we can't just build a fence around them. We need to bring them to the fence. How are we going to do that?" I asked.

"That is a problem. But even though I don't know how to turn around a herd of stampeding stegos, I am pretty excited to find out," Lin said with a huge smile.

I smiled back at Lin. It was hard not to when we were talking about a big adventure. But if I've learned anything in the Microterium, it's that getting a little advice before heading into an adventure is a good idea, too. I pulled my cell phone from my pocket and punched a button to video call a familiar face.

"Let's call the professor before you go cowgirling after the stampede," I said as the phone began to ring.

I swung around and tilted my camera phone so that the camera could see both of us. Professor Penrod answered, and before his smiling face was even in focus, Lin spoke.

"Howdy from the Microterium," she said.

"Howdy from Utah, Danny and Lin," he said.

The sun was shining around him, and I could hear a river nearby. His glasses had a new apparatus that filled my mind with questions.

But they would have to wait, because we needed answers about stampeding Microsaurs, not new inventions.

"It looks sunny there. Are you making any discoveries?" I asked.

"Certainly, Danny. This place is ripe with

dinosaur history, which makes it a prime location for Microsaur activity," the professor said.

"Cool," Lin said.

"Cool indeed, Lin. Now, how can I help you two this fine day?" the professor asked.

I told him about our near miss with the stego stampede, and how they were flattening everything in their path. Before I had finished, the professor looked very concerned.

"And that's not all. There's a humongous long-necked Microsaur with the herd of stegosauri, and he's smashing things, too," Lin explained.

"Oh, that'd be Wilson, and he's not just a long-necked Microsaur. He's an apatosaurus. A colleague of mine from Argentina is having me watch after him—oh, wait. I've said too much."

A hundred questions zipped through my brain at once. Did the professor have a friend in another country that knew about

the Microsaurs? Did this friend take care
of Microsaurs, too? Was there another
Microterium? I was about to start peppering
Professor Penrod with questions, when Lin
asked a question of her own.

"We were thinking about building a fence to
hold in the stegos. Do you think that will work?"
Lin asked.

"A fine idea. But don't forget. If you are going to put a fence around the stegosauri, you'll need to put it in a place that is just right for them. Lots of grass to graze, shade to enjoy, fresh water to sip. Fences are fine as long as what is inside is better than what is on the outside. Otherwise . . ." Professor Penrod said.

"The herd of stegosauri will smash it to bits," Lin said.

"Precisely," the professor said.

"Of course," I said as I made a list in my mind of everything the environment would need to be a perfect stegosaurus home.

"But there is one problem. Now that I think of it, a fence won't keep Wilson inside. No way," Lin said.

"Quite right, Lin. A fence wouldn't even be a challenge for an apatosaurus. I think Wilson will go wherever he likes. You just need to make him a place he really loves. I suggest a nice lake and plenty of company," Professor Penrod said.

"Like, more apatosauri?" I asked.

"Unfortunately, I'm not sure there are more apatosauri. Wilson is very special. I was hoping that he'd make friends with the stegosauri. I'm pleased to hear your report that he is traveling with the herd. He's friendly and protective, so if you can manage to corral the stegosaurus herd, I'm fairly certain he'll stay nearby. However, he will need a lake and loads of leafy food to eat, so that might be a bit of a challenge for you as well," the professor said.

"Okay, Wilson needs friends, water, and probably something to munch on," I said.

"That sounds perfectly patagotitanish," Professor Penrod said.

"Do you think he will like broccoli?" Lin asked.

"I'm sure he would. Who doesn't? In fact, I

believe he'd also like . . ." Professor Penrod said, then another voice spoke up from behind the professor.

"Professor. Will you come look at this, please? I think I've found something that might interest you," a woman's voice said.

"Certainly, Dr. Carlyle. I'll be right there," Professor Penrod said with a smile. "I've got to run. The science is alive and kicking here in Utah, as we had hoped."

"But wait! We have one more question. How do we get the stego stampede to get into the fenced-in area after we build it?" I asked, hoping to squeeze in one more question before Professor Penrod slipped away.

"Easy. You use the best tools in your toolshed. Your wise minds and creative imaginations," Professor Penrod said. "Be safe, and remember— adventure awaits!"

CHAPTER 3
SOUNDS LIKE TROUBLE

After our discussion with Professor Penrod, Lin and I spread out a large map of the Microterium on top of the die that we used as a table.

"So, we obviously need to unshrink," Lin said.

"Obviously, but I wish we had a plan for where to build the fence first. The grassy plains seem nice, but there isn't enough water. And the rolling hills behind the swamp are pretty good, plus there is the swamp nearby, which Wilson would love, but there isn't much shade. I just can't find the perfect place," I said.

"How about in the back corner in the red-rock canyons? They might like that area," Lin said.

"I thought about that, too, but it's too hot and sandy. It's basically a desert back there," I said.

"Maybe we'll just have to build something," Lin said. "We could dig a new lake and plant broccoli around it for Wilson. We could put it in a nice grassy area full of trees. You know. Make our own environment."

"That's what I'm starting to think, too. We could name the place Stego Valley and call the lake Lake Wilson," I said with a grin.

"Yeah, that'd be so cool. Let's do that," Lin said. "But first, let's unshrink. I'm not going to dig out a whole lake when I'm tiny."

"Good idea," I said. I pressed the button to get the Expand-O-Matic started. Before it would do its unshrinking trick, the machine that Professor Penrod invented needed to warm up. The purple Carbonic Expansion Particles had to get to just the right temperature to bring you back to normal size.

The Expand-O-Matic gurgled and popped as it warmed, but that wasn't the noise that caught our attention.

"I think that was Pizza," I said.

"No, it was Cornelia," Lin said. Then the moaning returned, only louder this time.

"It was both of them," I said. "Let's go check them out."

Leaving the gurgling Expand-O-Matic behind, Lin and I ran to the back of the Fruity Stars Lab 3.0. When we rebuilt the new lab out of the Plastic Interlocking Building Blocks that my dad and I had invented, we made sure to add a big window so we could look down into the playpen we had created for the twin Microsaurus rexes. We called the place the observation deck, and when we got there it was easy to see something wasn't quite right.

The toys that Lin had given them were torn to shreds, and there were little Microsaurus-rex-sized holes dug all around the place. Something didn't seem right. Pizza and Cornelia were usually happy and playful, but they were walking around inside the playpen, sniffing at the PIBBs and occasionally scratching in the dirt.

"What's wrong with them?" I asked. Pizza
looked up at me and groaned.

"Maybe they are hungry. They're growing so
fast that they may need more food," Lin said. She
ran to the food storage bin, opened the big door,
and pulled out a full slice of pepperoni so big it
looked like a blanket. "Help me with this, will ya?"

Lin and I carried the pepperoni slice to the

observation deck and heaved the big chunk of oily meat over the edge. It fell to the playpen, right between the twins. We used to give them small chunks of pepperoni, but watching them tear a big piece to shreds was so cool that we'd started giving them full slices.

The twins slowly walked to the pepperoni and nibbled at it.

"Where is all the tearing and shredding? That's my favorite part," Lin said. "It's like they grew manners or something."

"Hey, Pizza," I hollered down. "What's up? Are you feeling sick?"

Pizza looked up at me and smiled a little. He scratched his chin with his big back foot, then slumped down in the grass and huffed out a big breath of air.

"Corney. Whatcha doing, girl?" Lin asked. Cornelia looked up at us, then wagged her tail. She looked at it like she'd just noticed that she

had one, then chased it around in a circle a few times, like an overgrown puppy. She fell to the ground as well, softly chewing on her tail.

"They look tired. Maybe they need more sleep or something," I said.

"Oh no, Danny. It's much worse than that. This is bad," Lin said, which really got me worried.

"What? What is it?" I asked.

Lin looked at me with a very serious face. She cleared her throat, then spoke slowly. "Danny, I'm afraid the twins are bored."

"Bored?" I asked.

"Yes. It's quite serious. There is nothing worse in the whole Microterium than being bored," Lin said.

"Are you sure, because one time I fell from the sky while being carried by a flying pterodactyl."

"That was dangerous, but this is worse," Lin said.

"And if you remember, we were chased by a pack of hungry oviraptors while we were carrying a gigantic egg," I said. "That was much worse."

"Are you kidding? I'll remember that day forever. It's like one hundred times better than being bored."

"Lin. We were nearly flattened by a stego stampede today," I said.

"Even you have to admit that was better than being bored," Lin said.

I shrugged because she did have a point. "Yeah, that was pretty awesome. But still, being bored isn't the worst thing. At least the twins are safe."

"Sure, they are safe, but they are safe *and* bored. Every time I've been bored, I have ended up in trouble. Ask my parents," she said.

I had to think about it for a while. I didn't agree with Lin, but at the same time, I couldn't really disagree with her, either. Being bored was, well, it was boring.

"Well, what do we do now?" I asked.

"One of us stays here to un-bore the twins, and one of us goes and builds the fence. I think we know who the expert fence builder is here, so I'll volunteer to stay behind and play with Pizza and Cornelia," Lin said.

"That sounds like a good plan, but we better get rolling. We have a ton to do today," I said.

"Fine by me. I don't have a single thing to do today other than this. It'll be fine if it takes all day," Lin said with a smile.

"Well, the Expand-O-Matic is warmed up. I guess I'll unshrink and see you back here in a bit," I said.

"Sounds good," Lin said. I could tell by the sound of her voice that she was looking forward to playing with the twins while I was building the fence. And a little part of me—okay, a pretty big part of me—wanted to stay behind and play with the twins as well.

Just before I took the last few steps to zap back to regular size, my phone rang.

"Hello? Oh, I'm just fine. Sure. Hang on a second," I said into the phone. Then I called for

Lin before she had a chance to scoot down below to the playpen.

"Hey, Lin. I hate to tell you this, but I think our plans are changing before they even begin," I said.

"Why?" Lin asked.

"Because this is for you," I said as I held out the phone. Lin's shoulders slumped, and she let out a deep sigh.

She took the phone and started listening, and I could tell it wasn't good news.

"But can't we find someone else to watch her? I have an emergency to deal with today," she said, but even I knew the answer to that question. I motioned to Lin, waving, then jumped high and raised my hands over my head to try to look as big as possible. I wasn't great at acting games like this, but she got the idea. I was going to go unshrink and start building the fence. Lin shook her head and mouthed a big NO, while she waited for her mom to talk.

"Okay, I'm coming home. But can Danny come help babysit, too? He LOVES babysitting," she said, looking at me. I waved my arms and shook my head. I liked Lin's little sister, but I had a fence to build, and we needed to find a solution before the bored T. rexes tore the place apart. Plus, I still had to figure out a solution for getting the stegos in the fence.

Lin and I quickly expanded, but as we grew, I couldn't clear my mind. I had a lot of things to figure out, and I was pretty sure babysitting with Lin would not help me come up with a solution. There was an idea tickling at the back of my brain. I wondered if there was some way I could combine our T. rex issues with the stego issues, but I needed to do a little research before I was ready to share my idea.

"I can't. I need to run to the library to do some research," I said quietly to Lin. She brushed me off as she kept talking to her mom.

"Yeah. He said he can't wait. Thanks, Mom. I'll be home soon," Lin said. We walked through the secret barn-lab that was used as an entrance into the Microterium. I twisted the photo of Professor Penrod's first dog, Bruno the First, and a fake wall lowered in the back of the barn, hiding the Microterium from anyone who might get a peek inside.

"Good news," Lin said. "You can come help me babysit ChuChu."

"Um, yeah, I guess you didn't hear me. I'm not sure I have time for that today," I said as we jogged out of the barn.

"But you have to. If not, there will be three bored people in your life. Pizza, Cornelia, and ME!"

"You won't be bored. ChuChu is hilarious. She'll keep you busy," I said.

"Busy, yes, but I'm not so sure about hilarious," Lin said.

"I need to stop by the library first. I need to look something up. Then I'll go to my house and grab the PIBBs, and you can help me build the fence while you babysit ChuChu. How does that sound?" I said.

Lin put her skateboard on the sidewalk. "The library? That'll take forever. Every time you go in there, I'm afraid you'll never come out."

"Don't worry. I think I know what I'm looking for. It'll go fast," I said.

"I thought you said you were a slow-and-steady guy," Lin said.

"That's only when it comes to riding Microsaurs. When it comes to research, I'm lightning speed," I said.

"Fine. But stay in touch with me," Lin said. She tapped her finger to her ear, turning on the SpyZoom Invisible Communicator she was wearing. I heard a click in my ear as mine turned on as well. Lin kicked away on her skateboard, gliding down the sidewalk toward her home.

"Danny, can you hear me?" she said in my ear.

"Yup. Crystal clear," I said.

"Good. Then hear this. I'm going to make pancakes for me and ChuChu when I get home. You know that I'm the best pancake maker on planet Earth, and if you hurry, there might be a couple left for you, so HURRY!" she said as she zoomed out of sight around the corner.

"When it comes to pancakes, I'm faster than lightning speed. I'm Zip-Zap speed," I said.

CHAPTER 4

THE ANTI-BORE-ITORIUM

The city library is one of the oldest buildings in town. It is made of yellow-brownish bricks, has a statue of George Washington on the front lawn, and is surrounded by shady trees and nice places to read on a summer day.

I opened the door, and the smell of old books and carpet shampoo filled my nose. It was a nice, homey feeling, and my mind buzzed with all the things I could discover inside. Sitting behind an old wooden counter was the nicest person in town. I know because there was a town vote, and Mrs. Breen won in a landslide.

The librarian put down a book so large I wondered how she held it up in the first place. She smiled as she recognized me.

"Well, hello there, Daniel," Mrs. Breen said. She always called me by the name on my library card, even though nobody else ever did. Not even my dad.

"Hello, Mrs. Breen," I said.

"Are you having a good summer?" she asked.

"Yeah. The best. Hey, I was wondering if you had any books on training animals?" I asked.

"Sure. Plenty of them. Did you get a new pet?" Mrs. Breen asked as she started walking out from behind the desk. I joined her as we shuffled between the long bookshelves.

"Not really. I'm just interested in the topic," I said, which was true. The Microsaurs weren't my pets, and I was interested in learning more. Very interested.

"Well, you'll find everything you need on this shelf," she said as she led me down the aisle. "Anything you're looking for in particular?"

"I'd like to learn more about dogs that can herd sheep or cows," I said. I knelt and started reading the spines on the books. I was shocked how many there were.

"Oh, then I know the perfect book. I had a friend with a border collie once, and she trained him to herd her chickens back into their pen. It was the cutest thing you could imagine, and she said that the dog was so smart he practically learned it on his own," Mrs. Breen said.

The librarian traced her finger along the books until she found the one she wanted. She slid the book from the shelf and handed it to me. I turned it in my hand and was about to open it up, when I noticed a pair of eyes shining back at me for a second from behind the shelf. I leaned over to get a better look at the eyes, but they were gone in a flash. I shook my head to clear the thought, then turned my attention back to the book.

"*Training Ranch Dogs Lickety-Split,*" I said, reading the title out loud.

"The title has a double meaning. Not only does *lickety-split* mean fast and easy, but the dog in the book is named Lickety-Split," Mrs. Breen said. "I think you'll really like it."

"That's a great name for a dog," I said. I

flipped to a page in the book where a brown-and-white border collie wearing a red bandana smiled right at the reader. I was about to ask Mrs. Breen if she'd ever trained a dog, when a crash sounded on the aisle next to mine.

"What was that?" I asked.

"Just some books falling off the shelf. It happens from time to time," Mrs. Breen said. "Actually. I have something else you might like. Want to follow me to the DVD section, Daniel?"

The librarian whisper-talked as we walked, which was also one of the great things about Mrs. Breen. She might be the best quiet talker I've ever met because you can understand every word. I guess it comes with lots of practice.

"So, if you do get a pet, will you get a puppy?" she asked as we walked.

"I think so. I've always wanted one. My dad would let me get one, but I just want to make sure I know what I'm doing first. Do you have any pets, Mrs. Breen?" I asked in my best whisper-talking voice, which wasn't very good. I was afraid most of the library could hear me.

"I have goldfish, but they are lousy at herding sheep," she joked as we arrived at the DVD shelf. "Now let's see. Where is it?"

Mrs. Breen scanned the shelf, but she couldn't seem to find what she was looking for.

"Hmm," she mumbled. "I don't see it here. Let me go check in the computer and see if it is already checked out. Want to come with me, Daniel?"

"No. Thanks. I think I'll just go browse for a second. I might find something else, but I think this is the perfect book already. Thanks, Mrs. Breen," I said. I tucked my book under my arm and smiled.

Messing up my hair as she walked past, Mrs. Breen walked back to her post behind the desk, humming a little tune in her quiet librarian voice.

I waited until Mrs. Breen was out of sight because I wanted to check one more thing before I left, but this time it wasn't a book. Tiptoeing, I made my way out of the DVD area and back to the aisle next to the pet-training section where I had heard the noise. Sure enough, there were books spilled on the ground. I went in for a closer look and noticed a light dusting of purple glitter on the cover of one of the books. I picked it up and read the title.

"*Young Detectives Agency Presents: How to Spy Like a Pro, Volume 1*," I whispered to myself. There was something odd about the book, the glitter, and the little eyes I'd seen poking out from behind the shelf. Part of me wanted to investigate, but there were more important things on my mind. Like pancakes and stampeding stegosauri.

I hurried to the desk to check out my book, and while Mrs. Breen was helping me out, someone scampered out the front door. I turned to look, but all I saw was a blur of purple.

"Did you see who that was that ran out the door?" I asked the librarian as she handed me my book.

"Sorry, dear, I didn't," Mrs. Breen said. "Is something wrong? You look concerned."

"No. Everything is just great. I'm just seeing ghosts today, I guess," I said. "Thanks for the book. It's perfect." I smiled as I dropped the book in my backpack.

Mrs. Breen and I shared a wave, and then I hurried toward the exit. I took the steps in a single bound, my backpack bouncing on my back as I landed, and I started running toward my house to pick up a box of PIBBs. Then it was on to the next stop, Lin's house, where our work for the day had only just begun.

CHAPTER 5
A PLAN FOR PIZZA DOGS

Because I was carrying a box of PIBBs, I used my forehead to knock on Lin's door. It wasn't the first time I'd done it, and I was sure it wouldn't be the last.

"Come in, Danny," Lin shouted from inside. She didn't need to ask me twice because I could smell the pancakes from the porch and it made my stomach rumble.

"How did you know it was me?" I asked, letting myself in.

"Because you knock funny," Lin said. She was carrying a large stack of pancakes to the table, and she had a little bit of flour on her chin.

"My arms were full. What do you expect?" I said with a grin. I placed the box of PIBBs on the kitchen counter, then dropped my backpack to the floor and pulled out my library book.

Lin looked inside the box. "That's a lot of pieces. And is this what I think it is?" She held up a pre-built contraption that I had stuffed in the box before coming over.

"Yeah. It's a second Slide-A-Riffic. I thought it might be handy to have a few more in the Microterium for getting around a little faster," I explained.

"Hmm. Smart. And fun," Lin said as she wiggled her eyebrows up and down and grinned.

ChuChu, Lin's little sister, who was jumping on the couch in the other room, finally noticed me. I kept seeing her head bob up and down over the back of the couch, and every time she saw me, she waved with both hands. "Dan-nee! Dan-nee!" she said with each bounce.

"Hi, ChuChu," I said, calling her by her nickname. Lin had called her that since she was a baby. Her name was actually Chen, but ChuChu always seemed to fit her better.

ChuChu climbed over the couch, leaving a syrupy handprint streak along the back. Her shirt was covered with chocolate milk and butter, and her hair was stuck to her cheek on the right side of her face.

"She looks sticky," I said.

"She's always sticky," Lin said. "Come here, ChuChu." She was holding a dish towel in her hands, and ChuChu ran away, knowing that Lin wanted to un-sticky her.

"ChuChu sticky! STICKY!" she shouted as

she ran down the hall, and dove into her room headfirst with a crash.

Lin rolled her eyes and tossed the towel over her shoulder. "I'll catch her eventually. But you better eat before these get cold."

I helped myself to a couple of pancakes, then motioned to my backpack. "All right, I'll eat. You read," I said.

"Read what?" Lin said. Then she noticed the book sitting on top of my backpack. Her eyes got wide as she read the title of the book. "Oooh! Wait . . . ? Did you get a puppy?"

"Puppy?!" I heard ChuChu say from the room behind us.

My mouth was full of perfectly fluffy pancake, so after I swallowed it down with a gulp of milk, I answered, "No. No puppy. This is our research."

"About dogs?" Lin asked.

"Goggie?" I looked over my shoulder to see a sticky ChuChu leaning out her door with a curious look on her face.

"Border collies actually," I explained, then forked in another huge bite.

"Border collies?" Lin said. "Um, I like dogs and all, but where are you going with this, Danny?"

ChuChu started barking, then crawled on her hands and knees down the hall toward us. She woofed, stuck her tongue out and panted, then woofed again.

"That's right, ChuChu. Dogs go *woof!*" I said.

"These dogs are really cute," Lin said as she paged through the book.

"And smart. Smartest dogs in the world. Check out the first paragraph on rapid learning. I think its chapter three," I said. ChuChu crawled up to me and started rubbing her sticky cheek on my leg. I bent over and petted her head and she woofed again.

"Okay. I found it. It says, 'Border collies are best trained with affection and acknowledgment as a reward for good behavior. Treats work as well, but your border collie needs more than snacks. She needs love. Choose an action word for your new trick, something simple and short, then say the word. Next, show the dog the trick, or guide her into action. If your dog doesn't understand the action, repeat the word and try again. Once your border collie has completed the trick, reward her with a kind acknowledgment word or phrase, pet your pup, and, if she has been especially good, toss her a little treat,'" Lin said.

"Speak a command. Teach the action. Toss a treat," I said.

"Speak, teach, toss. We can do that," Lin said.

"I know, right? But check this out." I took the book from Lin and flipped to the chapter on herding. I spread the book out on the table, checking first to make sure the table didn't have as much syrup on it as Lin's little sister.

"ChuChu see goggies," ChuChu said. She held up her arms to Lin, giving up on her puppy act for the time being. Lin picked her up and plopped her down on the table next to the book.

"Look how these dogs work with their ranchers to gather all the sheep up. I only skimmed this book a little in the library, but it says that they come to it naturally. It's like they were born for chasing things," I said as I turned the page. "And look here. They look so happy and satisfied when all the sheep are inside their little pens."

ChuChu tried to touch the book with her carpet-lint-covered, syrup-smothered, butter-slathered fingers, and I pulled it away just in time. "Goggie go *woof*," she said.

"Great. All we need now is a border collie and a herd of sheep," Lin said as she used the damp dish towel to clean off her distracted sister.

"We can do MUCH better than that," I said with a smile. Then I looked at Lin and waited for her to put the pieces of the research puzzle together.

Lin looked back at me and squinted her eyes for a second. Then they popped open and she smiled wide. "Wait a minute! You're thinking the stegosaurus herd is like a herd of sheep, aren't you?"

I nodded and ChuChu *baa-aaa*-ed like a lamb. "And our very own Pizza and Cornelia are our border collies," I said. "Now you see why I was excited to do some research."

After cleaning up after our pancake feast, Lin started packing for our next adventure while I began construction on the stegosaurus fence. I needed four long pieces for the border walls, and

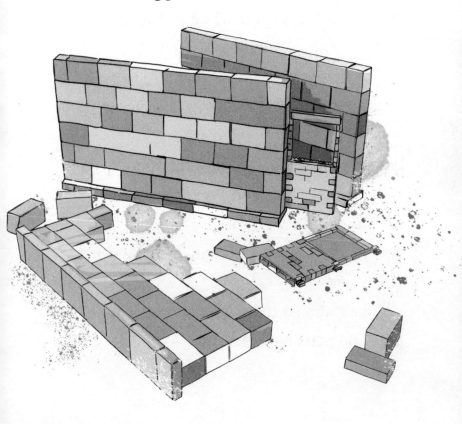

a big gate that would swing wide enough for a herd of stegos and a patagotitan.

It only took twenty minutes to get ready, and before long, Lin zipped my pack, then stood up and held it out to me. "We're ready. Let's go," Lin said.

I paused, not sure what to say. I knew we needed to get going to the Microterium to begin the training, but there was a problem.

"Lin. I think I should go back by myself," I said.

"What? Have you gone nutso?" Lin asked as ChuChu dropped the whistle and picked up a cake pan and a wooden spoon. She started banging them together and shouting "Nutso-Nutso-Nutso" over and over again.

"I just think, well, the Microterium is not the best place for a pot-and-pan-banging two-year-old," I said.

"She's almost three. And we can leave the pots and pans here," Lin said.

"I don't know. It's just not safe. And I don't want you to get in trouble. You are babysitting, after all," I said. I really didn't want to leave Lin behind, but I just worried that taking ChuChu into the Microterium was a recipe for disaster.

"Taking ChuChu on a field trip is very responsible. Fresh air is good for her," Lin said. "Ah, come on, Danny. You gotta let us come."

ChuChu chucked the pan and wooden spoon in the garbage, then turned to us and yelled, "Ta-DAAA!" It was a new thing she'd learned, and it always made me smile, even when I was trying to be serious.

"I think she could be a bit distracting," I said.

"We'll take her Snuffle Bunny. It helps her relax," Lin said. She picked up an old raggedy stuffed rabbit that was lying on the floor, dusted it off on her pants, then tossed it to ChuChu. The toddler caught it and ran out of the kitchen, into the living room. In seconds, we heard piano keys being smashed and some really strange singing.

"What is she doing?" I asked.

"She's playing her Snuffle Bunny song. See. Totally relaxing," Lin said with a grin.

"Umm, yeah. That's not very relaxing. I've seen fireworks displays that were more relaxing than that song," I said.

Lin gave me the saddest puppy-dog face I've ever seen. I sighed, not wanting to bring up my next concern, but knowing I had to.

"We can't have a two-year-old telling everyone about the Microsaurs. She hasn't even learned what a secret is, let alone how to keep one," I said.

This made Lin really think, but Lin thinks fast. In a flash, she raised her pointer finger in the air and grinned all bright-eyed, like she was holding the key to the biggest mystery ever made.

"We'll disguise them!" Lin said.

"Who, the Microsaurs?" I asked.

"Yeah, but not all of them. Just the ones that she might see," Lin said.

"Yeah. That's pretty much all of them, Lin," I said.

"No. Not really. I mean, we can tell her Bruno is a rhinoceros. And Twiggy and Zip-Zap, they are practically big birds. She'll totally believe that," Lin said.

"Big bird, big bird," ChuChu sang along with the piano-smashing song.

"She pretty much repeats everything I say, anyway. All we really need to disguise are Pizza and Cornelia. And maybe Honk-Honk if she even sees her," Lin said.

"And an entire herd of stampeding stegosauri," I added. "And about a hundred other Microsaurs that might sneak out of hiding."

"You're overthinking this, Danny. She's never seen a stegosaurus. We'll just tell her they are lizard-cows and she'll agree. Anyone who hears her talking about lizard-cows will just think she's making things up," Lin said.

"Oh man, this is crazy," I said.

"Crazy-awesome," Lin said. "I have some dog ears in my bedroom. Hang on. I'll be right back."

"Dog ears?" I asked, but Lin had already sprinted out of the kitchen.

"Goggie!" ChuChu said. She dropped to all fours, then crawled my way, holding Snuffle Bunny in her mouth. I worried the girl might actually turn into a puppy someday.

Lin was back in a flash, wearing one pair of the dog ears and carrying another in her hands. "See. When we get there, you hurry down and put these on the twins, and I'll distract ChuChu for a bit. Then we tell her they are big dogs, and she'll never know the difference."

"Lin big goggie," ChuChu said.

"Yup. Lin is a big, goofy goggie, ChuChu," I said with a grin.

"A big, goofy, *genius* goggie," Lin corrected. "Do we have a plan?"

I thought for a minute. Lin didn't look anything like a doggie, but Lin was correct, ChuChu repeated everything her big sister said.

"You have to keep her safe," I said.

"Of course," Lin said with a huge smile.

"And I mean really safe. Like protected like she's the most fragile egg ever made," I said.

"I have leftover bubble wrap from when my auntie shipped me that tea set for my birthday," Lin said.

"We're gonna need more than bubble wrap," I said.

"Don't worry, Danny. I know exactly what to do," Lin said confidently, and it was just the thing I needed to hear to convince me.

Convince me that we were making a huge mistake.

CHAPTER 6
GETTING DOWN TO BUSINESS

Thanks to ChuChu's wagon and Lin's skateboard, we made it back to the Microterium in record time. We slipped through the large iron fence in front of Professor Penrod's spooky-looking mansion, then ran through the deep grass to the barn tucked away in his backyard.

Lin darted inside the barn-lab and lowered the secret back wall to reveal the Microterium while I unpacked the box of PIBBs and ChuChu from the little wagon. I wanted to hurry and get us into the Microterium as quickly as possible because every inch of the barn-lab was covered in breakable glass jars, dinosaur bones, science equipment, and other fun things for ChuChu to smash.

I was about to make my way to the big metal step that turned on the Shrink-A-Fier,

Professor Penrod's incredible shrinking machine, when something rustled outside in the grass surrounding the barn. Normally, I'd just think it was a cat, but ever since the book-tumbling experience in the library, I had this strange feeling that someone was watching us. SPYING on us even. I poked my head back out the door to take a quick peek, but I couldn't see anything, or anyone, lurking around.

"Are you all right, Danny? You've been acting strange today," Lin asked.

"Sure. I'm fine. I just thought I heard something. It's just my imagination, I'm sure," I said. "Now, where were we?"

Lin was holding ChuChu on her hip and taping her toe impatiently. "We were standing on the big metal step, ready to shrink. You were staring out the door, looking for ghosts."

"Oh yeah. Sorry," I said. I stepped over the box of PIBBs, leaving them behind because I didn't want to shrink them, then made my way to the step with Lin and ChuChu.

Lin passed me the dog-ear headbands. "Don't forget to get these on the twins before you-know-who sees them," she said with a wink.

"Right," I said as the machine whirled to life. A shower of orangish mist sprinkled down on us, and in a second, we were all ant-sized again.

"OOOH!" was all ChuChu could say, yet I

totally understood how she felt. Shrinking in a flash really did give you an *oooh* feeling.

"To the Slide-A-Riffic!" Lin said.

She jogged, ChuChu still in her arms, toward a colorful contraption bolted onto the metal step. The Slide-A-Riffic was part roller coaster, part people mover, part terrifying.

"You're going to love this part, ChuChu," Lin said as she put her sister in the Slide-A-Riffic's travel basket. "It's super fast!"

"Oooh!" ChuChu said again. She had a hard time moving around with pillows strapped to her front and back, so she kind of toppled over, plopping down on her bottom, which made her giggle.

Lin jumped in with ChuChu. "Come on, Danny. Let's go."

The basket swayed back and forth when I climbed in. After checking to make sure everyone was ready, I pulled the lever to release the brake and the Slide-A-Riffic. It was slow at first, but soon gravity took over and we were flying down the cables that held the sliding cart in place.

The Slide-A-Riffic zoomed over the top of a small grove of trees, then whizzed down the cables as we sped toward the ground. I leaned back hard against the brake lever, and we came to a stop, a split second before we smashed into the ground. It was my best landing yet, and I smiled as the cart swayed and rocked slowly.

"Again! Again!" ChuChu said, bouncing up and down like an excited puppy in a bacon factory.

"That was fun, eh, ChuChu?" Lin said. She lifted her out of the travel cart and put her on the ground. "But you should have seen it before Danny ruined all the fun by installing brakes."

"Ruined the fun? I improved things. Did you not notice my smooth landing?" I asked.

"Smooth is for milkshakes, Danny. I'm more of a crash-landing kind of girl," Lin said, which might be the most honest thing she's ever said in her entire life.

"CRASH GIRL!" ChuChu said as she started running around. She smashed her fists together, then spread her arms in a fake explosion. "CRASHY-BOOM!"

"You two are weird," I said, but I couldn't help but laugh. ChuChu was exactly like her big sister. Built for adventure, and not afraid to show it.

We ran behind the Fruity Stars Lab 3.0, and I stopped as I reached the large gate that held the meat-eating twins in place.

"Okay. You and ChuChu wait out here for a second while I go check on our *doggies*," I said with a wink.

"Goggie?" ChuChu said.

"Not yet, ChuChu. Let's eat some chips first," Lin said. "We'll see the doggies later, isn't that right, Danny?"

I turned my back to Lin so she could get the bag of chips from my backpack. "Sure. Chips now, doggies later," I said. I pushed the tall gate open just enough to squeeze inside, then

shut it quickly before Pizza and Cornelia escaped the playpen. But it turns out, I didn't need to worry about that. They didn't even get up when I entered; they just turned their heads and smiled a little. There was no doubt—they were the most bored Microsaurs I'd ever seen.

"Hey, guys. I've got something for you, and I think you're going to like it," I said as I approached them, holding the fake ears behind my back.

CHAPTER 7
FOLLOW THE LEADER

ChuChu pretty much went bananas when she saw the twins dressed up like dogs, or "goggies" as she put it. She ran to them, gave them huge hugs, and started acting like a dog, too.

At first I was worried that ChuChu wasn't going to be helpful at all, but boy, was I wrong. The twins liked her as much as she liked them.

They sniffed her, which made her giggle, which made the twins very curious. After that, Pizza and Cornelia followed ChuChu around the playpen like she was their long-lost big sister.

Every move she made, they were right behind her trying to act just like her.

"Are you seeing what I'm seeing?" Lin asked.

"Yeah. I think so. Our training might be a whole lot easier than we planned," I said.

"Can I try something?" Lin asked.

"Of course," I said. I handed Lin the little bag of treats I had taken out of my backpack, and she gave me a wink.

"ChuChu. Sit, girl," Lin said, and her little sister sat just like a good dog.

"Woof!" ChuChu said.

"Good job," Lin said as she tossed her sister one of the pepperoni treats. ChuChu woofed again, then started to pant.

"Pizza, Cornelia. Sit!" Lin said. The twin Microsaurus rexes growled a little, looked at ChuChu, who was still chewing on her pepperoni treat, then they sat at the very same time and looked back at Lin.

"Good job!" Lin said as she tossed a snack to each of the twins.

"Oh my goodness. This is even better than the

training rules in the book. Let's try again," I said.

The training went slow at first. Even with ChuChu as our little example giver, the twins got distracted from time to time. But once they realized that it was fun to learn new things, they got the hang of it. After about an hour, Lin and I had taught them to sit, fetch, roll over, and stay.

But, it was only the first step in the process. We had to teach them to herd the stegos, and for that we were going to need help, and more volunteers.

"Hey, Lin. Why don't you get ChuChu and the twins to learn how to run in a big circle, while I go find us some sheep," I said.

Lin agreed and kept her training going. I squeezed out of the playpen gate and started looking around for Microsaurs to help us with the next part of the training. I found Zip-Zap, but I knew he'd be too much for the twins to handle. Then I walked around the front of the Fruity Stars Lab 3.0 and saw the perfect little group of Microsaur sheep.

Five squatty ankylosaurs were munching on some leaves and grumbling to one another. I'd spent a bit of time with them in the past, and aside from their spiny tails and tiny horned heads, they were totally harmless. I shooed them toward the playpen, then pushed the gate open and let them inside. The always curious Zip-Zap entered as well, and he squawked at Lin as soon as he saw her.

"Oh, hi, Zip-Zap," Lin said.

"Big birdie," ChuChu the girl said. Then ChuChu the doggie said, "Woof!"

"What do you think, Lin?" I asked. "Will these little guys work?"

"They're perfect," she said. "Bring them over here."

Lin and I had to pretend to be sheep to get the training started, but before long, ChuChu and the twins were able to chase the ankylosaurs anywhere Lin or I told them to go. Eventually ChuChu was so tired from all of her goggie make-believe that she was ready for a rest. Zip-Zap was sitting in the shade watching the whole thing, and his fluffy feathers made a perfect bed for ChuChu to take a little nap. She climbed on Zip-Zap's back and fell asleep while Lin and I kept training the twins.

Before long, the twins could herd the little group of anklyosaurs into any corner I pointed to. I'd just point, shout "Get 'em on up!" and the twins would do the rest.

"It is like they've been doing this their whole lives," I said.

"They are born herders," Lin said.

"Thanks to ChuChu," I said. "I bet Professor Penrod would love to see this."

I was about to suggest that we give the professor a quick call, when a loud SQUAAAAWK changed my mind.

Lin and I both turned back to look at Zip-Zap. ChuChu must have woken from a strange dream because she was looking bleary eyed and hanging on to two tiny handfuls of Zip-Zap's feathers. He jumped up and tried to shake ChuChu from his back, and when he realized it was no use, he sprinted out the door of the playpen.

We followed him out and up the little hill next to the Fruity Stars Lab 3.0. We got to the top just in time to see Zip-Zap bolt out of sight, zipping into the deep jungle grass.

"What are you standing there for, Danny?" Lin shouted as she ran after Zip-Zap. "Zip-Zap has ChuChu! RUN!"

CHAPTER 8
FOLLOW THAT ZIP-ZAP!

"Bruno! Help!" I shouted, and the trusty Microsaur charged into action. He ran right past me, shaking the ground with every step, and I swung up onto his back without him even slowing down. "Follow Lin!" I shouted as I pointed the way to go.

Bruno and I caught up to Lin pretty fast. She heard us coming up behind her, and she raised a hand as we went by. I grabbed her and pulled her onto Bruno's back with me, the extra weight not bothering Bruno one bit.

"They went that way," Lin said, pointing toward a small opening in a tall clump of bamboo. The grass was still moving where Zip-Zap and ChuChu had entered, but the Microsaur was nowhere in sight.

I turned Bruno's head toward the narrow gap, and the three of us barreled forward.

"The swamp is down there!" I said. "Zip-Zap hates the swamp."

"I know. Maybe he'll stop before he gets in the muck," Lin said.

Bruno crashed through the bamboo like it was made of wet tissue paper. The closer we got to the swamp, the more mud he slopped around. Soon it was a regular mud storm, but still, nothing could slow down our trusty triceratops.

It was hard to see with all the mud flying around, but I could tell there were hundreds of tracks smooshed into the soft earth all around us. The shady grass forest began to lighten up as we made our way to a clearing that surrounded the swamp.

I expected to see a Microsaur or two in the swamp, but I wasn't prepared for what I saw next.

The herd of stegosaurs surrounded Wilson,
the massive patagotitan. They were enjoying the
cool swamp, that is, until Zip-Zap *squaaaaawk*-ed
right into the middle of the herd, still carrying
Lin's little sister on his back.

Zip-Zap bounced, flipped, kicked, flapped, and half flew all around. Doing anything he could to keep his feathers and feet dry. The herd began to shift around, spooked by Zip-Zap's wild actions. Wilson slowly turned his massive head toward the noise, then roared a deep rumbling sound that made the swamp water ripple. It was as if the stegosauri were waiting for their boss to tell them to move because all at once they started to stampede again.

Mud, water, moss, and gunk splashed everywhere. Zip-Zap had seen enough. He bounced off the back of a particularly large stego and did an amazing double flip. When he was at his highest point, ChuChu slipped off and got stuck on the back plate of a stampeding stegosaurus.

ChuChu's little arms waved around, and while I couldn't hear her over the loud, splashing noise created by the swampy stampede, I could tell by the look on her face that she was loving every second of her adventure.

Zip-Zap flapped his wings so fast he looked like a cross between a hummingbird and an ostrich. He half fell, half flew over our heads toward dry ground.

"No! NO NO NO NO NO NO NOOO!" Lin said as she watched ChuChu being carried away with the stampede. "Chase them, Bruno!"

Bruno started through the swamp, but he was getting tired. We needed to do this smart, not fast, so I pulled him to a stop.

"What are you doing, Danny? We have to save ChuChu!" Lin said.

"I know, but we'll never catch her like this. Bruno just can't keep up," I said. "We need a plan."

"We don't have time for plans!" Lin said. "Let's GO!"

"You chase after them on Zip-Zap. I have another idea. Stay in touch with the Invisible Communicator, and we'll work this out. I promise," I said.

Without answering, Lin shot into action. She didn't slide off Bruno's back; she jumped, grabbed on to a flexible bamboo pole, then used her momentum to *twang* through the air. She landed on a surprised Zip-Zap, and in a flash, they were chasing after the herd.

"That was impressive, even for Lin," I said to Bruno, who grunted in response.

I pulled out my phone and launched the SpyZoom app. I didn't want Lin to think I was doubting her ability to keep track of ChuChu, but I had secretly slipped a GPS tracking device inside her helmet, just in case. Turns out, it was a pretty good idea.

The app located the GPS tracker and showed me on a map where they were heading. There was nothing but open prairies ahead of the stampeding stegos, so I knew Lin was in for a long chase. I tapped on my Invisible Communicator and heard Lin breathing hard in my ear.

"Lin. Just keep following the stampede. I'm going to expand and put the fence in place. We

need to be ready to corral the herd," I said.

"Hurry, Danny. These guys are faster than they look," Lin said.

"We'll be there before you know it," I said. Then Bruno galloped back toward the Fruity Stars Lab 3.0.

When Bruno and I got back to the lab, I ran inside, switched on the Expand-O-Matic, and sized up back to normal as soon as it was ready.

It was dangerous being regular-sized in the Microterium. I always worried, no matter how careful I was, that I might smash something really important. Even the plants in the Microterium are fragile. It had taken Professor Penrod years to build the perfect environment for the Microsaurs, but it would only take one big footprint by a clumsy nine-year-old boy to change everything. And it only got worse when you were in the biggest hurry of your entire life.

I made my way fast as a rabbit into the

barn-lab. The box of PIBB fence pieces was waiting for me on the floor where I had left it, but it wasn't alone. And neither was I.

I couldn't believe it was true, but I was staring into the eyes of a curly-haired girl wearing a purple glitter vest and a detective's hat. Vicky Van-Varbles, aka Lin's worst enemy, aka the absolute last person I wanted to see in Professor Penrod's secret lab, was staring back at me. But no matter how shocked I was to see her, it was obvious that she was much more shocked to see me.

She dropped a glass beaker she was holding, and it shattered as it hit the floor.

"You just . . . I mean . . . you were invisible . . . then you . . . umm . . . appeared in that . . . what the . . . huh?" Vicky's words sounded like they were falling down a staircase, bumping out in little spurts as they hit each stair on the way down.

I pressed the Invisible Communicator in my ear, turning it off for now. I was shocked to find Vicky in the barn-lab, but I was certain it was best to keep it a secret from Lin as long as possible. She had other, more important things to worry about.

"Hi, Vicky. Um, is there any way you can just forget all of this and pretend it was a dream or something?" I said, hoping that Vicky would forget that she just saw me expand from ant-sized to me-sized in less than a second.

"No way. Not a chance," Vicky said, her words sounding like they'd finished falling down the stairs and were now dusting themselves off, ready to run right back up again. She put one hand on her hip and pointed right at me. "You and Lin are up to something really sneaky. Probably illegal and horrible, too, and I'm not leaving until I've uncovered all the clues and know *exactly* what's going on here."

My stomach was in knots. Vicky Van-Varbles was *here*, and she wasn't going away.

And while I was standing there staring at her, a stampede of environment-smashing stegos was demolishing the Microterium, ChuChu was dangling from the back of one of them, Lin was following them on her own, and I still had to make a place for Wilson, install a fence, and get our herder T. rexes in place. There was too much to do and too little time. We needed help.

Lin was going to hate—and I do mean *hate* this. But . . . maybe we could use one problem to solve the others.

"So . . . um . . . how do you feel about dinosaurs?" I asked Vicky, and a little smile lifted the corner of her mouth.

CHAPTER 9
YOU'RE NOT GOING TO BELIEVE THIS

There was no way Vicky would believe me if I told her we were about to shrink to the size of ants, then hang out with hundreds of tiny dinosaurs. I mean, I wouldn't believe it if I hadn't seen it with my own eyes. I considered just shrinking her and letting her figure it out on her own, but I wanted to start slow, using science as my guide. But starting slow wasn't really an option when your best friend and her little sister were caught up in a stego stampede. I decided to work and talk at the same time.

"So, you expect me to believe that dinosaurs are not actually extinct," Vicky said as she helped me lower a ladder the professor kept around for just such an occasion.

"I know it goes against everything you have ever heard, but yeah," I said. We stretched the ladder from the floor of the barn-lab to the cement ledge at the back of the Microterium, carefully balancing it above the fragile micro-ecosystem.

"Well, I've never seen one," Vicky said.

I thought back to a few days ago when I was literally riding in a mint tin stuffed inside Vicky's purse with two Microsaurus rexes. She might not have seen one, but she had no idea how close she had been to a tiny version of me and two baby *Tyrannosaurus rexes*.

"Well, that's the tricky part. You see, after millions and millions of years, the few dinosaurs that survived began to lose their habitat to everything from floods, to humans building pizza parlors, to raging forest fires. So, to survive, they shrunk," I explained. I crawled out on the ladder, pushing the big box of PIBB fence pieces in front of me.

"Smaller. How much smaller?" Vicky said.

"Much smaller," I said. "Hand me that little hand shovel, please."

Vicky found the small shovel, then carefully teetered out on the ladder with me.

"So much smaller, that for millions and millions of years, nobody even knew they existed," I said as I inched out over the grassy plains area of the Microterium. I found a nice spot where a little creek was making its way through a tiny canyon, and I started digging.

"I know you're just making this up to make me feel dumb, Danny. It won't work," Vicky said.

"No. I'm not. Really, I'm telling the truth," I said. Then I saw something below me that would clear things up. One of the microsized anklyosaurs that we had used to train Pizza and Cornelia was chomping on a cactus so small it looked like a green speck of dust. I carefully picked the little guy up by his knobby tail. "Here. Hold out your hand. I'll show you."

Vicky looked at me through squinted eyes. I could tell she did NOT trust me one bit. After thinking about it for a few seconds, she slowly reached out her hand.

"Now, be careful. This little guy is fragile. Are you ready?" I asked.

"Ready for what? To play make-believe dinosaurs with you?" she said. Then she stuck her hand out toward me, daring me to change her mind.

I lowered the well-armored Microsaur into the palm of her hand. Then I waited as Vicky inspected the little critter.

"It's a bug," she said.

"No. It's an ankylosaur," I said with a smile.

"It looks like a bug," Vicky said. With the little critter balanced in her hand, she reached down and dug in the big purse on the floor nearby. Without ever taking her eyes off the Microsaur, she found a magnifying glass.

"Good idea," I said as I carefully lifted one of the pre-assembled fence sections out of the box. "Get a closer look. Make sure to count his legs. Remember, bugs have six, dinosaurs have . . ."

"Four," Vicky said.

"That's right," I said, feeling proud to be able to prove that I was right. "Dinosaurs have four legs." I put down the back section of the fence in the nice grassy field.

"And he's covered in spikes or something. Almost like a turtle shell with bones," Vicky said.

"Yup. Ankylosaurs are armored dinosaurs. Pretty neat, eh?" I said, placing the next-to-last piece down in the grass and connecting it to the others.

"Okay, I don't know how you did this. Here.

Take him back. I don't like lizards, even really, REALLY small ones," Vicky said. I looked over at her, and she looked like she was going to gag. "He's all gross and spiny. What if he gives me warts?"

I put the last piece of the fence in place, then held out my hand. She tumbled the Microsaur back to me, and I carefully placed him back next to his cactus. I was about to search for another Microsaur to show Vicky more proof, when it clicked in my brain that I didn't need to. In fact, I could just play right along, and she would think there was nothing in the Microterium except my PIBBs, a whole lot of dirt and tiny plants, and a single, super-spiny, very tiny lizard. I smiled real wide, knowing that I had nearly been trapped into telling Vicky our biggest secret but that I was safe.

"What?" Vicky said. "What are you grinning about?"

"Nothing really. It's just that you caught me. I was just goofing. There aren't any tiny dinosaurs.

You were right. Dinosaurs are totally extinct. There are only little lizards and bugs in here. That's all. Sorry," I said with a shrug of my shoulders.

Vicky stood up on the ladder. It wobbled back and forth, making me really nervous. "Sorry?

SORRY? You tell me this big lie to TRY to make me look dumb, which totally did NOT work by the way. Then all you have to say is . . ."

"Sorry," I said with another shrug.

"Aaaargh! You are so WEIRD!" Vicky said. She started to walk back off the ladder, and with all the teetering, she began to lose her balance. Just before she fell right into the Microterium, she saved herself from falling by taking a big jump from the ladder to the big metal step.

"Oh no! Run!" I shouted to Vicky as the Shrink-A-Fier turned on.

"Run? Why? Is a dinosaur going to eat me?" she said as a shower of tiny orange particles sprayed from the nozzle. And in less than a second, my biggest problem was half the size of an ant.

CHAPTER 10
WELCOME TO THE MICROTERIUM

I didn't have time to put the ladder back. Not only were Lin and ChuChu in trouble, but now Vicky was Shrink-A-Fied and alone in the Microterium. Well, not actually alone—and that would become an even bigger problem if I didn't hurry.

Before shrinking myself, I decided it was

worth the time to put the new, second Slide-A-Riffic in place. I put one end of the slide next to the Fruity Stars Lab 3.0, then stuck the other end up by the new stegosaurus fence. I had a feeling it might come in handy, and I've learned to trust my feelings in the Microterium.

I stood on the metal step, careful not to step on Vicky, and I stepped down hard. The Shrink-A-Fier sprinkled Carbonic Reduction Particles down on me, and in no time at all, I was her size.

I saw her before she noticed me. Her hat had fallen off, and her hair was all frizzed out like a cheerleader's pom-pom. I'd seen Vicky mad before, but she wasn't just mad. Vicky was furious.

I cleared my throat to get her attention, and she turned around and pointed a finger at me, her eyes wide and her eyebrows pointing to an angry V in the center of her face.

"You!" she shouted. "What have you done to me?"

"Hang on. I know this is odd, but you'll be fine. We just shrunk, that's all," I said.

"That's all? THAT'S ALL?! I have cake-decorating lessons in less than an hour. I can't decorate a cake if I'm smaller than cake-decorating sprinkles! FIX THIS NOW, DANNY! NOW!" Vicky shouted.

I stayed as calm as could be, then pointed

to the Slide-A-Riffic. "See that contraption over there? We're going to climb inside of it and zip down into the Microterium. Then I'm going to introduce you to a few new friends, who are totally safe. You're going to think it's so great that you'll forget all about cake decorating and being little because you are going to see the coolest thing on earth. But first, you need to calm down and trust me," I said.

"Trust you? The guy who turned me into an ant? Are you kidding me?" Vicky said.

I put my hands on my hips, copying the pose that she liked to use when she was in control. "You can trust me and I can show you something awesome. Or you can wait right here on this big metal step until I help my best friend rescue her little sister, who is currently in the middle of a stegosaurus stampede. Your choice," I said.

Vicky took a deep breath. Then she straightened her vest. She picked up her hat and put it back on her head.

"I am not going anywhere with you, Danny Hammer. I am going to wait right here until you tell me how to get back to normal. Then I'm going to walk—no, RUN—to tell everyone, especially my mom, who is the mayor of this town if you didn't know it, that you turned me INTO AN ANT AND TRIED TO SMASH ME LIKE A BUG!" Vicky shouted at the top of her lungs.

I backed away slowly, making my way to the Slide-A-Riffic. "Okay, suit yourself, but just to let you know, there are pterodactyls in this Microterium. You don't have to believe me now, but you will when they arrive. And if you think *you* like shiny, glittery vests, just wait until you meet Twiggy. My suggestion: Hand it over without a fight. Her beak is a bit snippy. And sharp," I said.

I climbed inside the Slide-A-Riffic and released the brake. "See you soon. Watch out for flying alligators."

The Slide-A-Riffic started gliding away, but before it rolled to the end of the step, Vicky started running.

"Wait for me!" she shouted, and I pressed on the brake lever just in time. She jumped inside, and the Slide-A-Riffic swayed back and forth.

"Glad you could make it. As Professor Penrod would say, adventure awaits!" I said. Then I released the brake, and we whizzed toward the Fruity Stars Lab 3.0 at a speed that would make Lin very jealous.

We landed with a bit of a thump, but I did use the brakes before we came to a total crashing halt. Vicky climbed from the basket and teetered around, a little dizzy from the ride.

"Well, what did you think?" I asked.

"I think you are trying to KILL me," Vicky said.

"Not even close," I said.

"Where are we? In the woods? I am not dressed for the woods, and there was something else that was wrong. What was it?" Vicky said dramatically. "Oh yeah. That's right. I'M STILL TINY!"

"We'll take care of that soon, I promise, but for now there's someone I'd like you to meet," I said.

Bruno was galloping our way, his big pink tongue slobbering out of his mouth. Vicky's back was turned to him, and I couldn't wait to see the surprise on her face when they met. Finally, some proof that even Vicky couldn't ignore. He came to a stop so close behind her I was shocked she hadn't noticed him.

"Turn around. Someone wants to meet you," I said with a grin.

"It better not be Lin. That's all I need, to be outnumbered by you two," she said.

Vicky turned around, and Bruno treated her to the biggest lick I'd ever seen. All the way from her belly button to the top of her detective's hat. Vicky didn't say a word. She just stared up at Bruno with wide eyes, then got all woozy and fainted right into my arms.

"Well, Bruno. Meet Vicky. She's usually a little more talkative than this," I said. Bruno licked her again.

I tapped on my Invisible Communicator, turning it back on to catch up with Lin.

"Hey, Lin. How are things going?" I asked.

"Not good! This herd is out of control! You better not be messing around. I need your help!" Lin shouted.

"I am helping. You just can't tell yet. Do you see ChuChu?" I asked.

"I think I see her, but it's hard to keep track. All these stegos look the same, and they're kicking up a lot of dust," Lin said.

"Okay. I'm bringing help now. Just keep following the stampede," I said.

Bruno looked at me funny, and I swear I could read his mind. "Don't look at me like that. Lin has enough on her mind. I'll tell her about Vicky later, but for now, let's go find that stampede," I said. Bruno chuffed a little bark in agreement. "I hope she can sleep through this. It might be better for us all."

Bruno sat down, and I leaned Vicky up against him. He sniffed at her and smiled.

"Okay, you two wait here. I'll be back in a jiffy," I said.

I sprinted to the playpen gate, then pried it open to release the twins. "Come on, guys, let's go find a stampede!" I said, and they rushed out the open gate so fast they nearly knocked me over. The twins danced around me, jumping up and down excitedly as they gnashed their sharp teeth together.

"Okay. Follow me," I said, then sprinted back to Bruno and Vicky. She was still pretty woozy when I returned, but she was starting to recover. I knelt down right next to her and tapped on her cheek.

"Vicky? Can you hear me?" I asked. She smiled, which was a nice change considering the last time she looked at me she wanted to tear me to shreds.

"Oh, hi, Danny. How strange to see you here.

I was having a dream that there was this huge dinosaur guy with three horns and he licked me. It was kind of warm, but mostly just gross," she said.

"Well, Vicky. I hope you're ready to hear this, because that wasn't a dream. He was real," I said. I pointed over my shoulder to where the twins were wrestling and growling behind us. "And so are they."

Vicky looked at the twins, and for a second, I thought she was going to pass out again. Then she focused and cleared her head, and the normal Vicky returned.

"We're still in the Micro-thingy place, aren't we?" she said, the little smile gone from her face.

"Yes. We are. And there are dinosaurs, Microsaurs actually, everywhere. If you can get past the fact that we're part of the food chain, then this place can be pretty cool," I said.

Vicky swallowed and thought about it for a bit.

"Listen, Vicky. I need your help. I know this is all a bit too much, but Lin is in big trouble and her little sister, ChuChu, well, she's in a whole lot more trouble. If you want, you can just wait inside that building over there." I pointed to the Fruity Stars Lab 3.0. "It's a nice place for you to relax, and as long as you promise not to touch any of the equipment, it is totally safe.

"Or you can come along with me and help me rescue Lin's baby sister. There's a good chance we could get stampeded by a herd of out-of-control stegosauri. We might get lost in the swamp or get pricked by a bunch of cacti. There's a pack of bitty oviraptors around here somewhere that are known to chase anything that moves. And I already warned you about the pterodactyls, remember?" I said.

"The flying alligators?" Vicky asked.

"That's right. The flying alligators," I said.

"We need to make a decision now. We need to really hurry. So, what's it going to be? Stay in that nice, colorful building and wait for me to return, or risk your life trying to rescue Lin and her baby sister?" I said.

Vicky thought about it for a few seconds, then surprised me with her answer. She stood up, dusted off her backside, then looked me in the eye. "Let's go rescue Lin's sister. If Lin gets rescued, too, that's fine by me. But I am not waiting all by myself in that huge toy building while you have all the fun," she said.

"Well. Okay. I hope you can hold on tight, because it's going to get a little bumpy," I said.

I nudged Bruno to stand up, then climbed on his back. I held out a hand for Vicky. "Come on. You're riding with me," I said, and I saw something on Vicky's face that I didn't expect. I could tell by the look in her eye that Vicky was enjoying herself. Vicky was ready for an adventure.

Vicky climbed up and sat behind me. "Hold on tight," I said, and she wrapped her arms around my waist. "Any questions before we take off?"

"Oh yeah. I have a lot of questions, but maybe just one before we go." She was looking over at the twins, who had noticed we were about to leave. "Are those dinosaurs wearing puppy ears?"

"Yup. It's a long story. I'll tell you on the way," I said. Then I nudged Bruno with the heels of my feet. "Come on, boy, let's go find the stego stampede."

CHAPTER 11
SMASH AND DASH!

I wasn't really sure where Lin, ChuChu, and the herd were at the moment, but before I could worry about them, I had to get check out the new PIBB fence I had installed. I knew exactly where that was, so I pointed Bruno in the right direction and we were off.

For the second time that day, I was riding double on Bruno. He smashed through the little trees in his path as we bounced along, and before we'd made it halfway, it was obvious that Vicky was NOT enjoying the whole experience. It was mostly obvious because she wouldn't stop complaining about it.

"Oh my goodness. Does this dinosaur do anything but smash things?" Vicky asked. She was holding on tight around my waist, but she kept sliding around as we bumped along.

"He crushes things, too," I said, half smiling to myself.

"Well, maybe you could try to drive him . . ." She paused as Bruno demolished a mushroom the size of a couch. " . . . around something once in a while. I think this is as much your fault as his."

I didn't respond. Honestly, I didn't have time to argue about how to drive Bruno. The longer it was taking me to help find ChuChu, the more I worried. Whether or not Bruno trampled down an old stick or two was not something I cared about at the moment.

The twins ran alongside us, their doggie ears flapping, and their powerful jaws clomping shut from time to time. They had grown so much since they hatched that they were almost as tall as Bruno now. Pizza dodged a stump that Bruno demolished, jumping so close to us that I could smell his pizza breath. Vicky squeaked, and her grip loosened a little, which made her slip down off Bruno's big rump and get caught in the curve of his tail.

"Stop! Danny! I'm going to fall off and die right here. Nobody will ever see me again! It's a near tragedy!"

Stopping was not part of the plan, but I did have time to reach back and give her a hand. I pulled her up next to me. "Hold on tighter this time," I said.

"Tighter? If I hold any tighter I'm going to—" Bruno jumped over a rock and slammed back down to the ground with a thud. "Ugh! What was I saying?" Vicky asked.

"I'm not sure, but hold on. This could get a little messy," I said as I steered Bruno toward a little waterfall. In between us and the stream was a gooey bank of soupy-looking mud. The twins entered first. The mud was so deep they were almost covered up to their tiny arms.

"No. NO. NOOOO! I'm wearing my best pink Brittany Belle Backcountry Bonanza Limited Edition shoes. They cannot get wet," Vicky said seconds before Bruno took a huge leap into the air.

Now, there is no doubt that Bruno is an excellent smasher and crusher. But I know from experience that his favorite activity is splashing. Especially if the splashing includes soupy, dark brown, kind of smelly mud.

The twins scampered out of the way, jumping into the stream that flowed from the waterfall, as Bruno came down like a cannonball into the muck. I would have to give it a full ten out of ten on the jumping-splashing scale, because just about every inch of us was coated in a thick frosting of mud.

I couldn't help but smile and shout out a big "ALL RIGHT!" because it was by far Bruno's best *kerplunk!*

"My Sparkle Diva Spring Collection vest! I have to send it to Paris to have it cleaned! It's practically RUINED," Vicky shouted through a mouthful of mud.

Bruno sloshed through the mud, splashed through the stream, then ran us through a waterfall car wash. The twins were waiting for us on the other side of the creek, panting and dripping with muddy water. They didn't look bored anymore; in fact, they looked as happy as I've ever seen them. I smiled, then turned back to look at Vicky before we took off again.

"That wasn't so bad, was it?" I asked.

She was so mad I think I saw some steam coming out of her ears and nostrils. "I am NEVER coming here again. EVER!"

"Well, suit yourself," I said, "but our adventure isn't over yet. You better hang on again."

Vicky squeezed me so tight I could barely breathe as Bruno chased the twins up a large grassy hill. The tops of the PIBB fence appeared as we got closer, and I was surprised—and a little shocked—to see how big the new stegosaurus corral looked.

"Look, Vicky," I said, pointing to the fence. "Remember that?"

"It's huge," she said.

"Actually, it is normal-sized. We're small," I said. I was really proud of how great the fence looked now that I was seeing it while tiny. It was multicolored, every color except red for obvious Bruno reasons. There were small gaps between the bricks, much too small for the tiniest of stegosauri to squeeze through, but just right for someone my size to peek through and get a good look.

Bruno took us to the gate, where the twins were waiting for us as they rolled around in the tall prairie grass, drying themselves off. The gate was twice the size of a garage door, and it looked nice and sturdy.

"All right, Vicky. Let's open the gate," I said as I climbed down from Bruno.

"All we do is work in this place. I need a break," she said. She slid off Bruno and tumbled to the ground with a thump. "You open the gate. I'll watch."

I rolled my eyes as I walked toward the gate. "Okay, Bruno. I guess it is up to me and you," I said. Bruno didn't hesitate. He followed me to the gate, and the two of us swung the door wide open.

After thanking my big, lovable smash-o-saurus, I walked back toward Vicky while I checked the GPS on my phone. She was still lying on her back in the grass, moaning and mumbling to herself.

"It looks like Lin and the stego stampede are pretty close. It's time to get the T. rexes into action," I said.

"Close to what?" Vicky said.

A low grumbling bellowed from over the hill. It shook the ground all around us, and Vicky sat up.

"Close to that," I said.

"What was it?" Lin asked.

"It's not a what. It's a who. Wilson, to be exact. The rarest and largest Microsaur in the Microterium. Perhaps in the world," I explained as I climbed back on Bruno. I whistled for the twins. Pizza and Cornelia ran around Bruno, ready to put their new skills to the test. "Come on. Climb on. We have to hurry."

Vicky looked up at me and frowned. "If you think I'm getting on that dinosaur again, you're crazy. I'm waiting right here," Vicky said.

"Fine. But when the stampede starts heading

this way, make sure to stay out of their way. I wouldn't want your Sparkle Diva Summer Collection vest to get smashed." I nudged Bruno, and he started to run toward Lin and ChuChu.

"It's the Sparkle Diva SPRING Collection vest. I can't believe you can't tell the difference," Vicky shouted as we bounded down the hill.

"Sorry. My bad. Watch out for flying alligators," I shouted back.

CHAPTER 12
GET 'EM ON UP!

As Bruno and I ran toward the stampede, I clicked the SpyZoom Invisible Communicator in my ear to get in touch with Lin.

"Hey, Lin. Are you there?" I asked.

"Of course I'm here. Where have *you* been?" Lin said. I could tell she was close to the herd of stegosauri because I could hear them mooing in the background.

"It's a long story. I'll catch you up later. Can you see ChuChu?" I asked.

"I've seen her a few times, but it's hard to keep track of her in the mess of stegos. They all look the same," she said. "I need your help, Danny. And I need it in a hurry."

"On my way," I promised, which was totally true.

Bruno, Pizza, Cornelia, and I reached the top of a rock-covered hill and looked down in a deep valley. Wilson, the gigantic patagotitan down below us, was surrounded by the herd. A dust cloud floated around them, and following along close behind was Zip-Zap with Lin on his back.

"All right, girl," I said to Cornelia, who was sitting right next to Bruno, ready for action. "It's time to shine.

"Lin. Holler for Cornelia. I'm going to send her your way," I said.

"Really? Where are you?" she said.

"Look up," I said as I waved. "We're just up the hill to your right."

"YAAAHOOOO!" Lin shouted, and it buzzed in my ear. "Come, Cornelia! Come help me, girl!"

Cornelia looked up at me, waiting for final instructions. "Go on, girl. Get 'em on up!" I said in my best cowboy voice.

Cornelia shot down the hill so fast she looked like a blur. She yipped and growled her happiest sounds as she burst toward Lin and Zip-Zap.

"What are you guys going to do?" Lin asked.

"Pizza and I are going to run to the front of the herd and see if we can turn them around. You guys are heading the wrong way, and I have a nice big fence ready for you behind this hill," I said.

"Holy Micro-oly! Cornelia is FAST!" Lin said. "She's almost here!"

"Come on, Pizza. Let's go bring this herd home," I said to Pizza, who looked like he was ready to burst he was so excited.

"Get 'em on up, boy!" I said, then pointed to the front of the herd. Pizza ran down the hill even faster than his sister, Cornelia. Bruno and I followed along, but he was growling and snapping at the herd before we were even halfway down the hill.

The stegosauri didn't pay a lot
of attention to Pizza at first, but it
didn't take long for him to convince
them that he was serious. All it
took was one serious ROAR for
them to understand that the young
Tyrannosaurus rex meant business. But
while Pizza looked like he was having a
blast, he wasn't doing anything to control
the herd. In fact, if anything, he was making
them run faster in the wrong direction.

"How is Cornelia doing?" I asked Lin.

"Um, she's having a lot of fun, but
there's a problem," Lin said.

"She's pushing the herd faster," I
said.

"How did you know?"

"Because Pizza is doing the same thing.
We need to make a new plan," I said.

"I think I see ChuChu. She's right in the

middle of the pack. But I can't get to her," Lin said.

"We need to get them behind the fence first. It should be easy to grab her then," I said.

"Okay. You stay up front with the herd. We'll be right there," Lin said. "I have an idea. Come on, Corney. Follow me!"

While we waited for Zip-Zap, Lin, and Cornelia to join us, Bruno, Pizza, and I kept trying to slow down the herd, but it was no use. Bruno nudged at passing stegos, but they were too big to budge. I shouted at the top of my voice, but with all the rumbling, they couldn't even hear me. Pizza was better at getting their attention, but the tiny carnivore was only scaring them into running faster.

"We're almost there, Danny. I can see a Bruno-shaped blur through the dust," she said. "Start running ahead of the herd. It's all part of my plan, and you know we're faster than you. We'll catch up for sure."

"Pizza! Follow me," I said, not bothering to ask Lin about her plan. When it came to making up crazy action plans, there was nobody on earth as great as Lin. Not even me. Not even close.

Pizza followed Bruno as we started to pull away from the stampede. I didn't realize how loud it was running with the stegos until we had pulled away a little bit. We kept running along, but I could tell Bruno was starting to get really, REALLY tired. But in no time at all, Zip-Zap and Lin caught up to us and she let me know the first step of her new plan.

"Follow me," Lin shouted as she turned Zip-Zap sharply to the left. I turned Bruno, and the twins followed us as we ran away from the herd.

I looked to my right as the herd kept going, running around a big swooping turn that looked like it would head back our way soon.

Lin was pulling away from Bruno and me, and I saw her jump from his back and land in a big flower bush up ahead on the big looping trail. She started plucking large orange blossoms from the bush. By the time we arrived at the flower plant, Lin had plucked about fifteen of the big blossoms and tossed them to the ground.

I jumped off Bruno's back as we slipped behind the flower bush with Lin. Pizza and Cornelia joined us, panting and smiling so big I thought they were going to explode with joy.

"Okay. What's the plan?" I asked Lin. She had pulled one of the flowers on over her hat and was stuffing her arms inside another.

"Easy. We're going to surprise the stego stampede," she said. She punched her arm inside another flower blossom, then waved her arms around and shouted.

I didn't mean to, but a little laugh snuck out from deep inside me. "Lin, this might be the strangest idea you've ever had," I said.

"Right? I know! Isn't it perfect?" Lin said as she stepped into a blossom, making her left

foot look like one of the big orange cones Mr. Albertson, the school janitor, uses to let you know the floor is wet.

"Of course. It's GENIUS!" I said as I jammed a big flower on Bruno's nose horn.

"Genius!" Lin said as she looped a big blossom on one of Zip-Zap's wings. Zip-Zap squawked. He didn't think the idea was as awesome as we did.

The rumbling of the stampede was getting closer as I pulled a flower around my waist. "Okay. I think it's time for the big surprise!" I said.

"Yup. On three," Lin said, and we both started counting.

"One . . . two . . . THREE!" we shouted together. Then the whole group of us, Bruno, Zip-Zap, Pizza, Cornelia, Lin, and me, all jumped out in front of the rolling stampede. The bright flowers we wore, combined with the massive ROAR we all let go at once, stopped the stampede in their tracks.

The herd was silent for a few seconds as they stared back at the strange display in front of them. Then Lin spoke up.

"I cannot believe that worked," she said with a little giggle, shedding her flower disguise.

"Me either. I thought we were going to be smashed pancakes for sure," I said.

"Wait. Look at that," Lin said as she raised up on her tiptoes. "Is that . . . ?"

"ChuChu," I said. She was hanging from the spiked tail of the stegosaurus right in front, sound asleep. All we had to do was climb up and get her.

I picked a handful of grass and fed it to the stego to help keep her calm while Lin climbed up to rescue her sister. The large Microsaur didn't seem to mind at all, but she sure did appreciate the grass, and she left me with a slobbery hand to prove it.

Lin walked along the stego's back, holding her sister in her arms. She hopped to the ground next to me, then gave her the most sisterly hug ever, and kissed her rosy cheek.

"Don't you ever leave me like that again, you little peanut," Lin said, and I saw a little tear drop from Lin's eye to the top of ChuChu's sleeping head. It woke ChuChu up, and as she blinked her eyes open, she smiled real wide.

"Sissy," she said, then reached up and pinched Lin's cheek.

"That's right. I'm Sissy," Lin said.

I didn't know what to say. I didn't want to rush anyone, but we still needed to get the herd back into the fence.

"Um, Lin. I hate to say this, but we still have some work to do," I said.

"Oh yeah. I can't wait. We have to get the stegos inside the fence, and this will be the ending to a perfect day," Lin said.

I was about to agree, when I remembered that Vicky was waiting for us back at the fence, and Lin had absolutely no idea that we had a visitor.

"Well, let's not say perfect just yet. You thought the stampede was shocking, just wait until I show you my little surprise," I said as I climbed back on Bruno.

"Oh, good. I love surprises," Lin said. She handed ChuChu to me, knowing that riding

Zip-Zap was a one-person job that took a lot of attention.

"Well, you're not going to like this one. Not one little bit," I said, then shouted to the twins, "Pizza, Cornelia. For the last time today, let's GET 'EM ON UP!"

Stopping the stampede took a lot of smarts and energy, but getting them going again was pretty easy. Lin and Zip-Zap went on one side of Wilson, and Bruno and I took the other. Lin and I shouted to Wilson, sending up lots of loud *Hi-yah*s and whoops until he started moving. After that, all we had to do was stay on either side of him and direct him up the hill toward the fence. The stegosauri pretty much followed along with Wilson's lead, but I sent Pizza and Cornelia to the back of the herd to make sure they all stayed together.

The journey to the fence started off slow, but before long, we were back to stampede speed once again. When we got to the hill, Lin saw the fence.

"Wow. That's humongous! Is that the surprise?" she asked.

"Umm. No. Sorry. I told you the surprise wasn't good news. That fence is very good news," I said.

Lin and I helped guide Wilson toward the gate of the fence. If we wanted him to go right, I'd move away a little, and Lin and Zip-Zap would ride close to his feet. Not wanting to squash them, Wilson would move a little to the right. And if we wanted to go left, we swapped. Lin moved away and I squeezed into Wilson's space. It was a little spooky riding that close to something with feet bigger than your bedroom, but as soon as we got Wilson through the gate, we were home free.

Lin and I were caught up in the stampede as the herd moved into the wide fenced-in area. The stegosauri followed Wilson all the way to the lake at the bottom of their new pasture before they stopped.

Wilson kept walking though, right into the

deep lake. His feet were covered first, then his legs. When the cool water reached up to his belly, the gigantic patagotitan let out another of his rumbling bellows. The lake water rippled with the sound and made waves that crashed against the shore of Lake Wilson. In a few more steps, the water was nearly up to his back, and he settled down and let out a massive Microsaur sigh.

"That was amazing," Lin said. "He looks so happy."

"I know, right?" I said.

"Was the lake the surprise?" Lin asked.

"No. Sorry, Lin. Actually, I don't see the surprise around here anywhere," I said as I looked for Vicky. I was a little worried that she'd wandered off.

"Come on. Let's go close the gate. It's been a long day," Lin said.

"Looooong day," ChuChu said as she rode in my arms.

"That is for sure," I said with a smile.

As we rode away from the lake, making our way through the herd of relaxing stegosauri, I had to admit the place looked pretty good. It was full of long, tender grass, and there was plenty of shade and fresh water.

"I think they are going to like it here," I said as we reached the gate.

"Is that the surprise?" Lin said as she slid from Zip-Zap's back. He ruffled his feathers and squawked. It had been a long day for Bruno and Zip-Zap as well.

"Oh man. I wish I didn't say it was a surprise. Remember, surprises aren't always good," I said. Bruno helped me and Lin shut the gate, and then ChuChu and I hopped off my trusty Microceratops and gave his nose a great scratch.

"Dino goggies," ChuChu said as she walked over to the twins. They were lying in the grass just outside the fenced-in stegosauri, looking as happy as I'd ever seen them. Their ears were still on, but they weren't straight anymore and they looked like they were ready for a nap.

"Well, Danny, if you don't have a surprise for me, I guess we better just head back. Maybe the surprise is no surprise," Lin said.

I was starting to worry about Vicky. She was supposed to wait right here for me to return. Losing a second person in one day in the Microterium would not be fun. Not one bit.

"Hey. You moved the Slide-A-Riffic," Lin said. "That's awesome. Now THAT has got to be the surprise." She took ChuChu in her arms and started skipping over to the Slide-A-Riffic. I was looking in the deep grass for Vicky, when I heard a scream.

Lin was looking down into the basket of the Slide-A-Riffic. "Vicky Van-Varbles! What are you doing here?" Lin shouted.

"Surprise," I said. Lin glared at me, and I shrugged. Nothing I could do now but explain, and I knew that might be the most difficult thing I'd done in the Microterium all day.

CHAPTER 14
SLIDING HOME

We used the newly installed Slide-A-Rific to make our way back to the Fruity Stars Lab 3.0. It was nice for two reasons. One, it was super fast, and two, Zip-Zap, Bruno, and the twins needed a break. Or at least that's what we thought. As we glided through the air, high above the ground, the Microsaur friends did their best to keep up under us.

After a smooth landing next to the lab, Lin jumped out of the Slide-A-Riffic first.

"Come on, ChuChu," Lin said. She held out her arms for ChuChu and helped her sister out of the basket.

Vicky climbed out next. Then I got out and followed Lin as she marched quickly toward the copper penny beneath the nozzle of the Expand-O-Matic. She put ChuChu down on the penny, then got down low so she could talk directly to her sister.

"You stay right here on this shiny penny, okay, ChuChu?" she said.

"Oooh. Is a BIG penny," ChuChu said. She was still hugging Snuffle Bunny tight as she plopped down on the penny, obeying Lin.

Lin looked over at me and pointed to the lab. "You. Me. Lab. NOW!" she said.

I swallowed, then nodded. I was going to obey Lin as well. I followed her into the Fruity Stars Lab 3.0.

"What about me?" Vicky asked.

I turned and motioned to ChuChu, then whispered, "Can you keep an eye on her for a while? We don't need her running off again."

Vicky smiled. "Okay. I like babies," she said.

"She's NOT A BABY," Lin shouted from inside the lab. I didn't know she could even hear us.

"I gotta run. I have some explaining to do," I said.

I found Lin in the control room for the Expand-O-Matic. She was leaning against a workbench with her arms crossed.

"So. How did this disaster happen?" she asked.

"It's a long story, but in short, she followed me here," I said. I hit the switch to warm up the Expand-O-Matic and checked the dials.

"I think you mean she broke into Professor Penrod's secret barn without getting invited," Lin said.

"Yes, but to be fair, that's kind of how we found this place, too," I said.

"Sure. But we were following a tiny-dactyl who stole your GPS beacon. She was being a snoop," Lin said.

I nodded, then looked out the front window of the lab. Vicky was sitting on the penny with Lin's sister on her lap. She was coating ChuChu's fingernails in bright purple fingernail polish.

"And then what? You just decided to shrink her and let her into the Microterium?" Lin asked.

"No, I didn't decide to do that. She jumped on the big metal step and Shrink-A-Fied herself in. What was I supposed to do?" I asked.

"I can think of one thing. You pick her up and put her in a bug jar. Problem solved," Lin said.

I heard barking and turned to check on ChuChu and Vicky again. They were obviously playing doggies because ChuChu was teaching Vicky how to sit and beg.

"That's not really an option, Lin. You can't just keep a tiny person in a bug jar," I said.

"You can if you're trying to keep the biggest secret on earth. We have like a bazillion secrets to keep? Do you think SHE can keep a secret?"

"Probably not, but we have to try to figure something out," I said.

"I'm telling you, Danny. There's a bug jar in the barn-lab. A bug jar will solve all our problems," Lin said.

"Still, not an option, Lin," I said.

I looked outside again, stalling for time as I thought about how to tell Lin about our next problem. Vicky took off her necklace and gave it to ChuChu, and in return, ChuChu handed Vicky her Snuffle Bunny. Vicky hugged the stuffed rabbit, kissed its nose, then passed it back to ChuChu. I had never seen Vicky act so nice. It gave me an idea. Even though she wasn't up for getting dirty, she did survive an adventure-filled day, which was a plus. And if there was a little bit of nice inside Vicky after a day like today, then my strange idea just might work.

Lin broke my concentration as I thought over my next steps carefully. "Danny, can we please try the bug jar?"

I half smiled back at her and shook my head. Something thumped on the ground outside. Bruno had made his way back from the stego fence, and he had found Vicky and ChuChu.

Vicky walked up to the big lump of horns and muscle and pretended like he knocked her to the ground. It made ChuChu laugh so hard that *she* fell to the ground as well. Vicky stood up and did it again, and this time all three of them fell to the ground, including Bruno.

"You know. She's not *all* bad," I said as we watched ChuChu and her play.

"Seriously, Danny?" Lin said with the biggest eye roll I'd ever seen.

"Well, ChuChu likes her. That's gotta count for something," I said.

"ChuChu also likes ketchup and crushed nacho chips on her peanut butter sandwiches. She likes everything," Lin said.

"I have an idea, but you're not going to like it," I said. "Follow me. We need to make a deal with Vicky."

"What kind of deal?" Lin asked.

"Just follow my lead, you'll see," I said as we headed out the door.

CHAPTER 15
LET'S MAKE A DEAL

Lin and I sat next to Vicky on the copper penny as we watched Bruno chase ChuChu.

"Your sister is really cute," Vicky said to Lin. "I always wanted a baby sister."

"Thanks," Lin said. "There are times when I'd give her to you, but most of the time she's pretty great."

"So. Are we getting out of here?" Vicky asked.

"Yes. Of course, but we need to work out a few details first," I explained.

Vicky stared at me like I was a talking alien. "Details. I thought you'd done this before," she said.

"We have. A bunch of times, but what Danny is trying to say is that we need to make a deal before we're going to let you out of the Microterium," Lin said.

"Oh," Vicky said. Then she thought about things for a minute. "Wait. Who says you get to choose if I leave or not? That's not fair."

"Oh, it's fair," Lin asked. "It's fair because we know how to make the Expand-O-Matic work and you don't. And if that's not okay with you, I know where there is this perfectly clean bug jar that we could use to—" Lin said.

I stopped her before she said too much. "Hang on, Lin," I said.

"A bug jar? For me? Oh, I don't think so," Vicky said, shaking her head snarkily.

"Hang on, you two. Give me a chance to explain," I said.

Lin and Vicky turned to look at me, and I knew I had better talk fast before they both ended up wrestling in the grass.

"Look. We're all going to expand back to normal. We just need to talk about a few rules first," I said.

"Rules. Like what?" Vicky said.

They both looked at me and waited for me to share my idea. ChuChu brought a totally slobbery Snuffle Bunny to Vicky.

"Fro to big rhino goggie," ChuChu said. Vicky smiled wide and tossed the Snuffle Bunny into the grass. Bruno and ChuChu chased after it, giggling and chuffing as they went.

Vicky turned back at me, ready to hear the deal.

"Here's the problem. Lin and I are afraid that if you go back to normal size you'll tell the whole world about the Microsaurs," I said.

"No, I won't. Why would I do that?" Vicky asked.

"Because this place is the coolest place you've ever been in your entire life and you'd become super popular if you told everyone about it," Lin said.

"Okay. That's fair, but I won't tell everyone. I promise," Vicky said. "And besides, what's the big deal if I told a few people?"

"If anyone finds out about this place, we won't be able to keep it safe. Reporters would come with video cameras and tell everyone about the Microsaurs. People might walk around in it, without knowing they need to shrink first, and smash—well, they would smash everything. And it wouldn't be fair to Professor Penrod. He's worked really hard to build this place and fill it with Microsaurs that need protection," I said.

"I won't tell anyone, I promise," Vicky said. "Cross my heart, hope to die." She drew an imaginary X over her heart.

"That's not enough," I said.

"Pinkie promise?" Vicky said, holding out a pinkie finger for us to lock and swear.

"Still. Not enough," I said.

"Well, that does it, then," Lin said, losing patience with the whole thing. "I'll go get the bug jar."

"There is another way, but it won't be easy," I said.

"I'll do anything. I don't want to be in Lin's bug jar for the rest of my life," Vicky said.

"The IMPA," I said. I looked at Lin and gave her a look that told her to play along. She did without losing a beat.

"Oh no, Danny. Vicky is not ready for the IMPA," she said.

"I know, but what choice do we have?" I asked. "And don't say bug jar."

Lin shrugged, and I could tell she was still voting for keeping Vicky in a bug jar.

"We can't leave Vicky in a bug jar. What would we tell her parents? They are going to wonder where she is soon," I said.

"They probably do already," Vicky said.

"We only have one choice. The IMPA," I said.

"What's the IMPA?" Vicky asked.

"What's the IMPA?" Lin said as if she knew exactly what it was and thought it was *crazy* that Vicky didn't know. "Go ahead, Danny. Tell her what the IMPA is."

"The International Microsaur Protection Agency," I said in my most grown-up voice to try to make it sound even more important.

"Sure. International Microsaur Protection Agency. Of course, but do you think she'll pass the test?" Lin said, making up some rules of her own, which worried me a little, but I went with it.

"Maybe," I said. "It depends on what is on the test this time."

"Oh. I just looked up the rules yesterday. There are four tests in total. Bravery, Food, Questing, and . . ." Lin paused as she tried to think of another test. I jumped in before she thought of something really dangerous.

"And the Promise Keeper's Oath. You have to memorize it," I said.

"Oh yeah, that's it. I don't know, Danny. I don't think she's ready," Lin said.

"I'm ready. I could do that. What do I get if I pass the test?" Vicky asked.

"You get to come back to the Microterium with us," I said.

"Once every other year for fifteen minutes," Lin said.

"We can work on how often later," I said.

"Great. We have a deal. Let's expand and shake on it and forget this whole thing ever happened," Lin said as she stood up. "Except for the stampede part. That part was pretty cool."

"Well, not so fast," I said. "There's one more thing."

"Oh, good gravy. What now?" Lin flopped back down on the penny.

"Vicky has to stay at your house tonight. She needs to be with one of us until she passes the IMPA test," I said.

"Nope," Lin said. "That's impossible. The whole deal is off."

"Sorry. She can't stay at my house. Maybe ChuChu can keep her company," I said to Lin.

"Fine," Lin said, "but this will not be a glittery

199

sleepover. No fingernail polish and makeup experiments."

"Can we at least watch a movie and have some popcorn?" Vicky asked.

"Maybe. But only if it's a scary movie," Lin said.

"I love scary movies," Vicky said.

Lin looked at Vicky like she didn't believe her. "Really?" she asked.

Vicky nodded her head. "They are my favorite. Have you seen *The Moth Man from Moon Island*? I was afraid of butterflies for a whole week after I saw that one," Vicky said.

"Okay. It's settled," I said. "Grab ChuChu; then you three stand on the penny. I'm going to hit the go button on the Expand-O-Matic. We'll be back to normal in no time."

As I stood and walked away, Lin asked if Vicky had *The Moth Man from Moon Island* movie, and I knew my plan was going to work out just fine.

When I got inside the lab, I poked my head out the little window.

"Oh, and I may not be staying for the whole sleepover thing, but you bet I'm coming to watch the Moth Man movie. I'll bring the popcorn," I said, which made all of us smile.

"Deal," Lin and Vicky said at the same time.

"Deal," ChuChu said, and I pushed the go button and then sprinted out to join them on the penny.

A MESSAGE FROM PENROD

"It was nice speaking with you earlier about your situation concerning stampedes and stegosauri. I trust you were able to work things out, as usual.

"I must say that I've hit the Microsaur jackpot. The Utah desert area is so rich with dinosaur opportunities, both old and new, that it is truly a paleontological playground.

"We'll be packing them up soon and sending them to you and Lin at the Microterium.

"I was glad to receive your update about the fenced-in area for the stegosauri and the natural canyon lake you crafted for Wilson. Perfectly prodigious ideas both. We've discovered so many new species of Microsaurs and new plants that finding inventive ways to section off areas of the Microterium will certainly come in handy. It will be easier to ensure the safety of the leaf-eating Microsaurs from South America, if we can keep the razor-clawed raptors from Utah in their own little space.

"Dr. Carlyle is beaming with excitement to explore the Microterium when we return early next week. She's hoping to find a volunteer or two to help dig holes for her new plants. I told her I know just two to ask.

"Well, I must be off. Dr. Carlyle and I are

taking a river trip into an area that hasn't been visited by humans in thousands of years.

"Oh, and one last thing. Last time I was in the Microterium, I noticed the Expand-O-Matic's Carbonic Expansion Particle fluid was running low. Keep an eye on it, and I will refill it the moment I return.

"We'll meet again soon, and remember. Adventure awaits!"

FACTS ABOUT STEGOSAURI

- Stegosauri were massive, plant-eating dinosaurs from the Jurassic period, which means they lived over 150 million years ago. They have been discovered in North America, Europe, and, as Professor Penrod learned, in China. In fact, one of the first confirmed findings of a member of the stegosaurai family was Huayangosaurus, named after the town where it was found, Huayang, China.

- Stegosauri were large and heavy dinosaurs. The largest of the species could grow to more than thirty feet long and weigh ten thousand pounds.

- While they were very big, their brains were pretty small. In fact, a fully grown stegosaurus had a brain about the size and shape of a hot dog.

- One of the most recognizable traits of the stegosauridae family is the long, bony spikes. These spikes are called thagomizers. The term *thagomizer* started as a joke from a *Far Side* comic by Gary Larson, in which a group of cavemen are being taught by their caveman professor that the spikes were named after "the late Thag Simmons." The name has since been accepted as the official anatomical term. Thanks, Gary!

- Fossils discovered in the Morrison Formation, a very important dinosaur bone site in Wyoming and Colorado, inform us that stegosauri really did travel in herds. Over eighty stegos of different ages were discovered in that site alone.

ACKNOWLEDGMENTS

This book was a rush to write. Sometimes the ideas came by the hundreds, rushing in like . . . well, like a stampede, I guess. Actually, at one point, I had no idea how I was going to wrangle all the crazy thoughts and notions into just this one book. It was a madhouse, no doubt.

But, like most adventures, things go better when you have a friend or two along to share the load. This bookish adventure is no different.

I know I sound like I am on repeat here, but I couldn't have corralled this herd of words together without the help of my wonderful editor, Holly West. Oh, and her trusty troop of book bandoleros, Liz Dresner, Emily Settle, Jean Feiwel, Heather Job, and the rest of the crew at Feiwel & Friends.

Then of course, there is my agent, Gemma, whom this book is dedicated to. Who has proven time and again that book friends are the best friends of all.

And most of all, my family. With them in mind, I have truly won the jackpot. Jodi, Tanner, Davis, Malorie, and Annie, you are my everything.

And in the end, I have to thank my readers. The Microsaur fan club is growing and opening up slots for new members of the IMPA. I hope you're ready, Jack and Michael. I know they are ready for you.

DUSTIN HANSEN, author of *Game On! Video Game History from Pong and Pac-Man to Mario, Minecraft, and More* and the Microsaurs series, was raised in rural Utah. After studying art at Snow College, he began working in the video game industry, where he has been following his passions of art and writing for more than twenty years. Dustin can often be found hiking with his family in the same canyons he grew up in, with a sketchbook in his pocket and a well-stocked backpack over his shoulders.

MICROSAURS

BEWARE THE TINY-SPINO

COMING JANUARY 2019

Thank you for reading this **FEIWEL AND FRIENDS** book.

The friends who made

TINY-STEGO STAMPEDE

possible are:

JEAN FEIWEL, Publisher

LIZ SZABLA, Associate Publisher

RICH DEAS, Senior Creative Director

HOLLY WEST, Editor

ANNA ROBERTO, Editor

CHRISTINE BARCELLONA, Editor

KAT BRZOZOWSKI, Editor

ALEXEI ESIKOFF, Senior Managing Editor

RAYMOND ERNESTO COLÓN, Senior Production Manager

ANNA POON, Assistant Editor

EMILY SETTLE, Assistant Editor

LIZ DRESNER, Associate Art Director

STARR BAER, Senior Production Editor

Follow us on Facebook or visit us online at mackids.com.
OUR BOOKS ARE FRIENDS FOR LIFE.

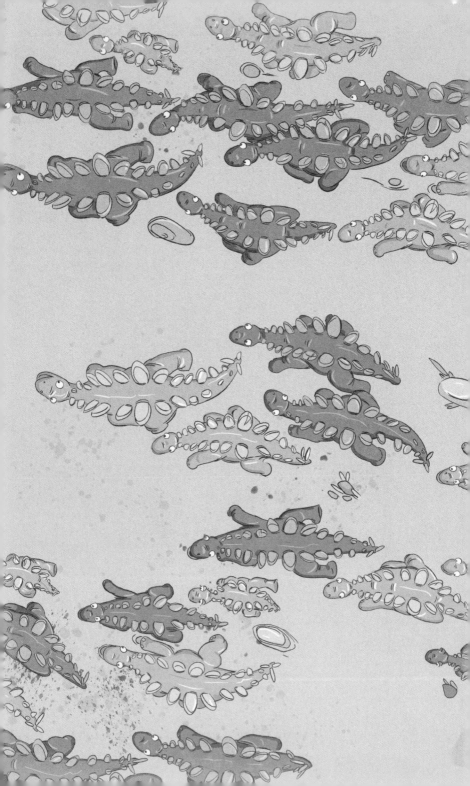